MOTION OF THE CYPHER

Recent Books by Ray DiPalma

The Jukebox of Memnon

Raik

Night Copy

5 Ink Drawings 5 Poems
[with Elizabeth DiPalma]

Mock Fandango

Metropolitan Corridor

Numbers and Tempers

27 Octobre 29 Octobre

Hôtel des Ruines
[with lithographs by Alexandre Delay]

Symptoms of the Absolute

Platinum Replica
[with drawings by Elizabeth DiPalma]

Provocations

MOTION OF THE CYPHER

➤

RAY DIPALMA

ROOF BOOKS
New York

ISBN: 0-937804-61-4
Library of Congress Card Catalog Card No.: TK

Author photo by Elizabeth DiPalma.
Cover design by Deborah Thomas.

The author gratefully acknowledges the following publications in which versions of some of the poems collected in *Motion of the Cypher* originally appeared: *American Letters & Commentary, Avec, Caliban, Central Park, Disturbed Guillotine, Exquisite Corpse, Five Fingers Review, Grand Street, Hambone, Hole, Hot Bird Mfg, Infolio, Juxta, Lingo, The Little Magazine, Motel, Mudfish, New American Writing, North Stone Review, O.ARS, Oasii: Broadsides, O-blek, Prosodia, Ribot, Salt Lick, Shiny, Stele Broadside Series, Talisman, Washington Review, Writing, Yefief; From the Other Side of the Century: A New American Poetry 1960-1990, Postmodern American Poetry,* and *50: A Celebration of Sun & Moon Classics.*

Thanks to The New York Foundation for the Arts for a grant that was of help in writing the poems in this book.

This book was made possible, in part, by a grant from the New York State Council on the Arts and the National Endowment for the Arts.

Roof Books
are published by
Segue Foundation
303 East 8th Street
New York, New York 10009

Let Tel-harsa rejoice with Aparine Clivers.
For Cipher is a note of augmentation very good.

Let Rehoboam rejoice with Polium Montanum. God give
  grace to the Young King.
For innumerable ciphers will amount to something.

Let Hanan rejoice with Poley of Crete.
For the mind of man cannot bear a tedious accumulation of
  nothing without effect.

Let Sheshbazzar rejoice with Polygonatum Solomon's seal.
For infinite upon infinite they make a chain.

-Christopher Smart, *Jubilate Agno*, FRAGMENT C

for Elizabeth DiPalma

CONTENTS

REBUS BALCONIES

The millionth billionth summer approaches from the West
prancing around a hoop of cloud the hackwork of sunrise
the season's still over the shoulder where tension keeps
its own diary on telegram paper yellow green and black

A billionth billionth day with a forehead of pavement
down the street comes the raw foam of readership
filling the by-lanes with the utility of its odors
disabused of the apocryphal before the noted wheel

A billionth trillionth hour thunders among the pears
as time passes hyper-polysyllabic point to point
scoring the sans continuous with the ancient G force
to bring more of the same blossoms in an air bottle

A trillionth trillionth circuit transgresses the corrosive
moments and somas wig-wagging to the disinterested
shoe-filled trees the words to the song with bees in
the handle dry mottos and banners today out on the isthmus

REBUS FEAST

Hobo nickel a modern gong laudanum's curfew
Buglewort in the halvah Sumerian Chelsea dogs
Where the seven manages is sonnet form
Lynx shadow across the sundial for starters

Lace dainty the tideline where the moon
Does its part for sloppy-dollars Gainsborough
Who got the idea from Blister Marjoribanks
When the weight fell the canvasbacks floated

Paradise extracted and earthworms in the jigsaw
A further statement on pale green paper
Where the six functions is the rose

Crack your rhythm fast rubber snap it
A smooth blue stone into the beano
Radius eye in wintergreen cools the blast

REBUS TACT

Sinking into sound grief
Is no penalty but the humdrum
Not to be shared but placed in
A basket and lifted over the walls.

Or there's the telephone . . .
What's not to be read is face down—
Its traditional imagery fills up
With unfamiliar shadows if properly abstract.

Nice salvos for the farm lads and professors—
Subtle black and white pictures of
The brick stacked a storey high in some
Places and a little less in others.

It should be plainly noted that when struck
Properly with a small metal mallet this brick
Will chime crisply and resonate into a
Lulling hum after a moment or two.

Descended, tolerant enough, how long is
A moment or two? How red is red? How empty
This advice? In the cavern you understand how
A shadow works because you've brought your own light.

But once out in the sun which way should you face?
Standing still, perfectly still, at noon and
Then turning quickly on your heel you might be
Able to figure it out without asking someone.

An experiment with a curl of smoke, perhaps . . .
There's a way to measure time in that.
Nothing too obvious would be special enough
Unless an engine could be rigged to run on it.

It's always the old matter of would and could—
The issues of could and would. No point or notion
In a costume migrating from a vast design could
Or would be well-enough intentioned. A matter for

The recuperative powers of patient groping
And the prudent indecisions that minister to
The definition of a proper sense of distance—
A dog barking off in the barn, a mystical stroke.

REBUS ARCHIVE

The trail is brown and blue.
Asperities . . . collective
Instructions, wavelengths,
Places of instruction with
Nothing else to do but accumulate
The papers and assess their
Pockets of successful nostalgia.
The transparency of the immaculate
Not its broken promises still
Gives work to the minions of
Cold devotion and dependent exaltations.
Their plodding hours with further
Possibilities—pale explanations,
Congruent distractions, the imagined
Dartings of rhythms never heard
Before the stacks and reams began to form.
A special series of folders for arguments,
A drawer full of the serpentine half-triumphs
Where the sentences began with a hollow
Question almost elastic in its perfection
Of spiraling candor and acceptance of
Imaginary feeling framed by the genitive.
Truculent erasures, irreproachable elaborations,
Telescopings, foliage full of ether . . .
Protracted passages almost successful in
Their search for an untempted vocabulary
Fixing its stare on the darker sincerities
Spoken of and emptied of any presentiment.
The purple back and forth trailing off
Into white . . . the declamatory confusion
Rising out of acquiescence and the fragile
Contract cut with self-reproach.

REBUS BRAG

I come from a remote mill town
At the foot of Bouquet Hill
Down river from Tarentum
Sleep was cactus in the grit
Pikelights in the alleys
A place of names in polyglot
Few theories more clang of hammer
To pipe and whine of winch
Sugar slopped into coffee
Factory roofs and broken windows
An interrupted sky sirens at all hours
Pungent chemistry man and river sweat
Voices loud as the wind in the weeds
Reaching back unanswered some and
Shaped elsewhere in the fragments
Declined in furthest emphasis
Declension of shapes sweetest
Sourest sounds salted voices
Drums and rainbow dust
What is the lost to the gone
But another night

ON THE MOEBIUS

Day and night the navigation leaks dust
Out onto the parrot weir
Tidal no room to walk

Tavern cello principles
Walking down big in a clean shirt
First the glass is wet then cold then full

Ophelia drafts pulling up short
Like threats dissolving into property
Guide star green and blue no exception

Blows distance no it touches me
With inland accents flat enough
To amplify the nebulae

A quick question which far
How one
Make it two

Night and day the navigation makes way
Filling the up with the way around
And the how with both

INTERRUPTED VERSION

Temperatures by plain
Austere inches
Violins and three hours sleep
Le lea le lee the lie les less and less
Plain austere pikas
Temperate as the inclination runs
The words start over together
Surmise designed in a drift
In lonely answer to some foreclosed radiance
Busying the eye

No and yes as illustrated
By the thoughtful straight man who
Owns the alternatives
Entrepreneur of the formerly anyway
Unremarkable but baffling

The copy firecrackers around the babble
A sympathetic warning instead of the usual humjob
Bit of glower in the afterburner maties
Snarls shine down on the clucks splashing in the myth
Bees to rotate the ephemera
The pressures of scorn and excuse
Ancillary to raw information
Exploit the noise by division
Word by word line by line at least

WHEN DID YOU FIRST REALIZE
WHEN DID YOU START TO REALIZE
WHEN DID YOU FIRST START TO REALIZE

Conversations with perfect strangers
Perfect ones hoota hoota hoota fresh air
I'm for that and lumbering quasi-primitive realism
At least for a few miles

Muted trumpets and phony saxophones at night
A badly drawn thick line from A to 3
A vast slope of clarity ending at the back door
Just another priority established to take hostages

Putting it all together makes you
An ambassador to Baghdad
Desperate circumference (remember Stalin
And what was made of him in the 50s)

For a conjunction
In an alley full of cash
Cat spray and pale shadows
East of the indolent dolors

NO MAN MUSIC

A hoax of clamor crawling with ambition
Or just another busy day

All spotted-out with detachable accomplishments and
The kind of hostile generosity that bleeds detachment

The grim look of books from 20 and 30 years ago
Nothing more forgotten than something that grew

From 70 to 500 pages only once a man was dead
Calculations the earnest shufflers made winding

Down to addenda and monograph
Better paper licked with crisper type and fat margins

INDIGO SHIFT

Blizzard of æons razing
the pathology of gape

Time honored ensign

Ancient of ancients
spooling the white hole

Lost illusion
of the irritable absolute

Who to salute

BELLY WHISTLE

Celestial kinked partings
Vegas Vargas Partagas
Pantages Pantaloon Jack's back
Where the scowl propounds aches per pound

Xenophon mumbles it's the thirties
Wide stride and in the element
Solar charm and shithook drapeau

Corn of Elysium
Firkins accoutred with acoustics
Gloomy thunder just the same

Laurels hang from the linear
There's Charlie Fumble Dollars
He thinks he remembers

Something Oppenheimer said
But he don't remember jackshit
He took a bite out of the common darkness
And called it his fortune

ALL THE SIGNS WERE RIGHT

Phantasy bijoux
Wine chants
And amen cramp

Mind find behind
Rhapsodies of gazing
A hawk drifting into the that-a-way

Leafing thumb of pliant aptitude
It's a stubborn pathos
Undulate in prelude

First death's pantomime rescue of presto
Pure static
First comes the curious and central mutter

Pure static purest simmer
Flagging the hour
Monotony's extra o

Locust canticle and banjo
By banjo default after default
Serif to cockade and epitaria

Collect (noun) to collect (verb)
For the hour to hour rouged for Sunday
Target yellow target red target

HOWEVER APOLLO

To that be all
Will that be for now

Not on one but on this
One on this one is all

Masonry answers masonry
That enlarges all at large

A little red that howls
In the dazzle that howl in time

That change beyond the obsolete
That diction absolute that absolves
To be all that
To be that is all now furthered

That intricate that choice
That Ur that obscure resemblance

Eye of gratia that no deduction
Can be made in harmony that shape then

Adornment beyond that fracture of integers
That participation that debt

That wadi that savannah that panicle
Drum cage of the trickle

ATLANTIC STRIPE

As undefined as a period of transition
Not waves
The apoplectic and apologetic
Course of the coast
Workplace and meadow and the indulgence
That falls between
A brightness
A chamber of fetched and found
Adzed symmetries
Not justifications
Directed emotions enlisted as an afterthought
Plains of frost form's candor
Or the cunning box hollow for palm
To raise its plangent code
Needs and scope in hard-to-find sequence
The altitude (pitch) and solitude (resonance)
Of italic edges the thinnest blade
Wafer and paper wafer and arrow
Both and all lined up along the function's fold
Like a spill of birds spiked on the wind
See the broadcast proven
Not its urge
To cast a chapter-minded net
Inscribed on a pillow
Over the numbness of the arm
Where the head might rest and catalogue
What the lips first shaped
Not the tongue or breath
Performed clarification for persuasion
Performed clarification unpersuasive as performance
But as clarification as persuasive success
Eye to eye
Do to me what you read
Do not read to me what you do

THE CONTIGUITIES

The corked bottle
And trug of fruit
The glass knife and
Starched blue cloth
With its pattern
Of stars and moons

QWAT

Repeat
the tetralogy
of taradiddles
they could always
be heard again

Four into five
gives one more
just to strike
the balance
with the disgorged

The hand played
on the knuckles
minus the com-
promise valor
always demands

Gravity is
the privilege
of foot where
balance is pleasure
2+3 minus on-

Five is four held
in place by a fifth
in angle binding
the count in rows
of one to one

A FABRIC OF CAPITULATIONS

Eager changes outside a diversion
conform to the intermittent and crept-upon

I scratch my head above the book
of red dots and black bars

An amazing sameness tangled
in the practical is put to use once again

Tomorrow and tomorrow and tomorrow
still only brings us to Wednesday

Longer breaths instead of predictable
distances are what are needed

Not stamina pulled by the hair but
the unanchored margin of anonymity

A place ready to assume its surface
rather than erase what first stood in its way

APRILVILLE

The weather fits itself around the human edges
The way it shapes the leaves and trees
Most instructive as is the waiting

Everything in the garden
A shattering of fruition
So called because of its classical origins

Antiquity and its branchings never
To be eluded but never to be more
Than the spirit of names and changings

The scholar reads
I give you this dirt broken into flowers
The words become stones in his mouth

He takes them off his tongue
And arranges them by size across the page
Alternating large and small with large and small

Soon two maybe three rows are formed and
Lines of blue and red ink connect the varied
Pairings until a loosely-rendered grid appears

A natural arrangement articulate of one or more
Aspects of gratitude gives first a shape to consider
Then one to make plans against or within

Though the temptation not to break the order
Is difficult to overcome in the garden
One can't wait to make a harvest

BURNING BRICKS

What is Hecuba to him
Or he to Hecuba
When he makes the cut
It's Hecuba to me
And Hecuba to him

I see you see
I see you seeing the edge
Walking in the wild
Thought water to fill
The map of landscape
Stashed among the foretold
Newspapers and crimson gases
Instead of responsible sentiment
Mare Crisium and the lion for luck
That's where to go but not an answer

It's just the whisper you can hear
Priam Hector Paris Troilus
The whisper above a whisper
What is this to me
What is it to you

Excuses
The rain's expensive
The rain's expensive all right
The day's rival leaves through a hole
Excuses through a hole in the roof

The edges are hot
Hot enough to break your heart
No smoke just fire
Just fire like a knife just fire
Fire on the rain

A WATERMARK AND A SCAR

And after the reinvention of part
Of the missing plan what
Is left but praise and intuition
To share to cut a piece of both
And place it on the page with
The careless patience of 46 years
Held in the tangles of an afternoon
Its music furniture newspapers jugs and loaves
Become a landscape sleeping and dug deep
Into the stammering tact of written interventions
Sleep's hold on the tongue makes
A shout impossible an animal groan
Rolls off the slackened jaw instead
Of the words that would ask
Are you there is that you on the steps
Answer are you there who is reaching
Through the locked door answer

AS FOR AND IS WHEN FOR HOW AND WHOM

It's time to be darker and lighter
More and more like the keys of the piano
Nothing to open or close but plenty
By which for which and with which to reckon

A lasting sequence no matter how random
Not a system not a series and certainly not
A system and series of sequences
The eyed-out one to one no plus or and involved

Not a trap for nostalgia's buzzing luster
Nothing to be made way for no axe to grind
No theoretical droolings that would confuse
Plod for permanence or projectile for project

Small plots and gestures in small books
Half-asleep violence and nonchalance agog
Could be strategies or stratagems or just next
An ordinary if evasive degree of starting over

A map an easel painting a drawing a watercolor
A torn bit of canvas and its interesting ravel of thread
In one corner or all in one corner or the guignol of
Assorted torn and neatly cut photographs

Brought up from some innocent and mannered
Geography to be a record of
Not what is there
But what it sees

SYMPTOMS OF THE ABSOLUTE

Systems and versions leave the pattern
With laughter to release the accommodated
The latter so named to disguise its
Exploitation by the interpretive secret

This is a void by distraction
All that can be done is wait with words
Remastering the previously determined
And turning it into an unimpeded disclosure

The moon follows the sun
Could it be suspicion makes the argument
Unapproachable at its most characteristic
East admits West

Could it be what the summary touches
Outside the focus of its immediate context
That could be it of course
Looking for the distant and intervening resolve

SAID LOOKING

The order simultaneous
One one the order to one
One to one logick's leap and slur
Later phrase incorporating
Muscle strain with 20-20 vision
Chemistry a balance of salt
On the tongue in the brain
On the bird's tail for muse move
From door to window to chair from
Chair to desk to window to door to
Bed to window to chair to desk to door
Come back come back and the bird flies
Content with furthermore and
What and means

COLOR IN TIME

All is
any other
than I've known

Words colonize
meaning and
vice versa

Sinking
colonies
and sinking colonies

Not tick tock
but tic
talk

Even if
or arguments
and then even if

Darkness comes
to sweeten
the breath

Portent
pour tension
poor ten pour ten

The infinite to be
two
one and the same thing

TWO NOTES ON A SOUND

1.

An (almost)
vertical
eagerness

almost
inquired
to sing

watching how
and where
the words

end up
Shanghaied
and barked

afoul of
the beam
tongue

under the
horizontal give
go and got

2.

Boxed by
the cry
climbed
to the stop

a wall
then

boxed (held)
by the ear
cry (the walls)

the stop
holds
facing
the wall

no
exit

boxed clouted
by the cry
held at
the stop

a wall
then

a wall
and a
way out
not over

MOTION OF THE CYPHER

Accepting
the seduction
fosters
the once organized
imperfect
outside
that was the model
of center.

Not focus
but the turned-to
culled from
the eliminated
and balanced—
a pejorgraph
of choice and
limn.

The sprawl
before
and the sprawl
after balanced
outside
of language
and inside
the pattern.

To be taken so
in the hush
of impulse
and worth how
is it done
to be done
to the order
and its shiver.

SMALL ELEGY

for Asa Benveniste

Gaunt frequency
and splintered touch
grey paper and
the wavelength of words
this morning and those
mornings remembered
loops of dust between
the motions driven by
and within the limits
of since plains of versions
dead oaks filling
these venereal leisures
and neon cavities
called sacred towns
of the caravan words
for the clumsy memory
its hands held out
cupping the wind
the same pressure
that pulls the tears
makes the emblems

LINES FOR E

My different
my difference
speaking itself
looks into
a corner another
corner to reflect
its light and smoke

The rest advances
space here measured
by the brooding
and traffic
of diction without
the prescient smoothness
of outward weld

Down to the rust
and lighter lines
confluence and hyphens
the birth and dates
of style and the vectors
of its spiral trans
spike to smudge

For example
for example
determining the thaw
uncoiled careful
to explain
the nothing different
in the active difference

ALL RIGHT I MEAN OF COURSE

The emperors wore out the circumferences
With their inscriptions and I would do the same
As it's come to me in this spot along the tumbled frieze
What was it they wrote Come back come back
Duplicity and deception it symbolized nothing
A request to be heard just once more just another
Adopted voice with nothing to celebrate

SOMEWHERE SELF NOWHERE ELSE

Nothing decorative rather
a hybrid of what is found
and slowed to a verbal pace
for the purpose of being numerous

Some red and white would
be of use here and some violet
and orange and black and yellow
for the farthest reaches of occasion

I have else by deletion at my side
a thaw and a stepping-aside
should the electricity fail there's
nothing but separateness to negotiate

A paraphernalia all right
squared with the totems and banners
where the stare takes its autonomy
and simulates a dazzle of surmise

Just looking after all just having
a squint at the loosely crowded and
soon to be lost watching the vacant
provide blank circumstance for guarantee

28 SEPTEMBER MCM90

Punned what in the eerie Jeru to Salem
First day of a new year making its grace on the eyelid
Its rise and fall Babylon to lower Broadway
Knotted geist of the Nthgram
Scribble and scuff of the gentian
Concoction of paradigms that wither on the name
Chic of the Hydra and Ho extending the word
Made mandarin guerrilla to braille with the panther
Here's the dark lobe here's the shy chic of psychic
Ein guter Kamerade ein guter Meester Meister Salud
Herr Goldthroat Herr Geltbeutel Herr Fragemicheins
Since the invasion I've cut back sharply
Cobble of the saracen spaced for Mr A Mr Thus
Known now to the few as Mr A or B and who are you
I only ask because I'd like you all to know
People of the frontier people of the icon and fact
New-suiters new suitors new sooters new Suters
"Yes, we had one—a damn fine specimen too, I might add,
Nicely painted, red, as I recall—out there alongside
The white chickens before the fucking wheel came off . . ."
Mes amis mon ami Ms. Amy you legatees of the price-makers
Who early developed their ways and thoughts for us

MAKES SPEAK

Legion legion legion legion legion legion legion
Angle loop egg over egg speckfloat bar hole mound
Legion legion legion legion legion legion legion
Silence and similitude in a non-discursive space
Set out upon the mirror to compliment the exclusion
Of decor hybrid rebus of horizon superimposed
On its own light not the eyes' moted beam

By minus to retrace the share that's left
By speculation and vamp the first poise
As clearly seen the shadows cast
Mimetic precipitate hung with the weight
Of its flawed shape and enjoined articulation of edges
Legion legion legion legion legion legion [legion]
Only **thought** on the topic by reflex to polis

TAPED SHUT

Writing behind the inhabited flow
Soft touch on the W hard on the T and D
Not so much tongue and tooth as lip
And throat W to W bright with I and E
And a monochrome A and O in the tether

Water steppes to the tune wall
Dividing ear stare from ear stare
Hot branch to hot branch for cheating the riff
Punctuation from the hole to negotiate the felt
From the first version on

The arrow will not show neither the council it gives
But to be had in the way of it all
Conned and inflected with Murphy Winch Conn and O'Reilly
Themselves turned into bicycles and traps
As though anyone cared what they rode around on

MASQUE OF THE ENGRAVERS

The crouch of shelter and an ikon of particularities
One wit of judgement and two more steps to the edge
Waiting who would not turn to resist this splinter of
Obvious temptation to lethargy and curious dissatisfaction
Safety is full of the sound of grinding incognita flashing
A soft green light to signal the process is underway
There it goes while a bell rings twice indicating another
Error in procedure has been made manifest and it's
Time to stop hit another button once or twice and start again

APROPOS CERTAIN DISCLOSURES

Voices call the sawed-off that couldn't stop
Stationary ones made to leap through credible
Positions voices around holes of laughter
Choices by either wandering through the turned
Setting to curve not down by much and endowed
With speed and agility but betrayed by same and context
The small word we finally agree on changes much
But like the white words that were introduced to
Replace any possibility of error they were mere
Diversions and proved to be unequal to the task
At hand and were wasted on all except those who
Could count to the pattern established after the rhythm
Of the reactive intricacies of line could be felt
Where it began likes wings against the window

AN INCH OF OPTIMISM A MILE OF RIGOR

On the hard lips of the sentinel
Chewing on his paradox
Down come the snows of November
Let it come down he remembers
The waiting and watching
The candle in the distance
The only light that fills the eye
In meditation a pre-Socratic phantasy
Held against the cold
Despair and cynicism are on the other
Side of the wall facing the wind
Snow fills the chinks melting and freezing
As the sun comes up and moves behind the clouds
In a cadence of ceremony
The weight in the step of his goal fills
The measure with the measure to wait

GRIFFOLINO D'AREZZO & CAPOCCHIO

Word into money the alchemy of debased coinage
Terms of the term of baser . . . no mettle—only
Mock metaphor the Kupfernickel in the nickel
Still more of the same from the little grifters
And strunzi with heads like cabbages nourished
On their own κακ and paid by the month
To talk about it . . . Be now disabused of any sense
Of process employed . . . all is appropriated
And selective to profit full of droll hunchings
That would pass for humor—beetles in the bread
And piss in the soup that's offered you
Make no mistake about it when you stand
In some dank tavern or shithole of a lecture hall
Something is not something else nor is it like
Anything that would bring the taste of the dollar
To what perplexes or consoles

CRADLE MENAGERIE

To make tributary of one more word

Balanced on appearances
And tamed by conjured irridescences
The here and there of the sun and clouds
Points of departure reconciled
With furrow ditch and cave

Dust spirals in the scattered rain

Levers pylons bags of air
Signs ingots derricks barrels
Of kerosene pulleys chains vats
Yards of plastic and metal tubing
Piled on pallets

An apple in an oval on a slab of stone

IN HARBOR

The mysterious within the embrace
And its immaculate flicker
Two arms when one would do

The foot frozen in coincidence
With minor distinctions involved
My foot your coincidence

The water is wild beneath the kite
Is that Han Shan at the end of the string
Or just someone's version of him

In response to a lost poem
No we are not sorry the leaves
Have fallen so we turn the page

The powdery residue at the bottom of
This box says it was once a well
This unwrinkled discipline will not enthuse a race

White-capped lurchings over the stink
Of the blue miles or in blaring variance
Happy as orange plaster set with diamonds

All the tricks in order of facility
Red plumes green clouds the formula
Always and only in black

BEAR NET

The angle formed is
At a distance
By the strings of a written page
Turned straight to the naked edge
That lures but doesn't cut
A cold and shaken slouch to the right
Pulling the web tighter
Against the wind
Harmonic ply against ply
The lines of the webbing cutting
Across the face

A STRANGE MENAGERIE OF GOLDEN MONSTERS

Ardent harmony
So many delights
Where among
Makes one one
Of the gang one
By one compounded

Bright with
A little con-
Sideration with
What the stars
Shine up not
Down up on

Dispersed a beat
To scan the accuracy
Nothing skimped to
Include but who
Put these here for
Those of them

To be
Those
Of them

WHITE CITY

Calculating the predatory
that fragments from one face
to another repeating together
I divide I make up for the zero heat
across the alabaster circuits and upright
stones of the city I divide I make up
for the white chalk trails of the walls
so cold and abstract in the face of the sun
I divide to hold the limits held in trust
seen to want confounded in the pretense of means
like a desert where little enough remains of what
was once more candid the smoke and breathing
cobble is now a place of spoken silences
and departures another echo I divide the riddled
with the passing the abraded with the lost
there are no weeks or months or years only days
lost in the eyes who speaks who divides who counts

ON THE MEND

A little better
than worse
than ever

Tomorrow and
tomorrow
and tomorrow too

Only the shadow
is complete—
made of its parts

Seated, Etruscan:
consolation to whom
is capricious—and piney

A discharge of hymns
in the distance: shit on
the old shoes of aspiration

21 DOWN

I continue nothing I
Am the author I sit in front
Of the last and the lost I offer
No distinct images glinting steadily
And bending closer and closer
Their wet rhythmic torpor
Making a bid for landmark status
Ornament under the grainy blackness
Of another phrase beginning 'Of . . . '
Books are everywhere colossal
Half-triumphs every one part formal
Agreement part ultra-sensitive acquiescence
And non-discovery lost in curiosity
Gaining in forgetfulness and in time to ask
Who said "Much that is beautiful must be discarded/
So that we may resemble a taller/
Impression of ourselves . . . "?
Recording the words on a scrap of
Note paper crossed with blue lines
Nearly an inch apart . . . veins of the record.

POEM

Pinpoint or star
The sigh is hollow
A perfect spark
With which to lance
An aura or repair
A distortion

Principle—the form
That surrounds the mirage
And inside that
Which comes to seem
Rude but not careless
In its sameness

The commission of something
In combination to be
Neutral in reflex un-
Guarded then bleeding its
Surprise no better that way
Or worse construing a bankrupt heretofore

Parts of the same to whistle
At qualms and make amends
For the one answer that frames
Itself again as a question Who
Listens asked from the worshiped
Intoxicated unreachable changes submitted

The reach expended to be
Ultimate or upturned or unpunished
The pensively wide apart as thunder
And lightning figments of supposings
And interventions to make mystery of
Which came first the sound or the flash

FOUR PART INVENTION

Surmise forever
what's been flattered
and flattened
by heart

Wheels inside
wheels out
a side of silence
aside

One out one
in to be in
balance—vulnerable—
and/or able

This day begins that day
began—obliging something
departed and unuttered in a
flourish of detail and decay

WATCHING THE MOUNTAIN BURN

Walking and talking
and charming, taking a
part of the path to the con-
ducive and conducting self
first and foremost, let me
tell you a little about my-
self upon your self just let
me hold a bit of your ear
on my tongue your broken
teeth on my fingers minding
how unmindful this balance
of going can strike any smaller
human agency just passing through
on the way to the mirror on
the way to the window on the way
to the door to the window and mirror
plenty of as well as no good reason
antidote to the best of both walk
with a limp don't cry out when
the teeth come down and
the tongue is cold and dry

COMMOTION

for Betsi

To me you look up where I
look up where the ceiling meets the
wall—there's one—but in here it's
being viewed at 200% instead of a pad
of paint on the end of a pole
all edge for the wire that runs the
join to make the angle that cut me
a line of sight packed with small shadows
ten pages better than only ten lines
given to the inventory of angles
made possible by the late March
sunlight play against the brickwork facing
south come 4:30 of a more pliant afternoon
than I deserve to record by putting common
measure to your uncommon grace and patience

TWO POEMS FOR PAUL CELAN

1.

Neck of the beam
cast from
the thickest bone
and scratched
nichts zum nada
for hair
       totem
not the he
of whom
but this facepost
points in ponder
at the moon
and humbles the sun

2.

Ten's a ditch
and by tens
or tens and threes
turned in loops
above the tight lariat
we come to Celan's
river face first

Elegy greeted
beyond the inched
ache of cobble
and rain for skin

Thin horns
so alarming

Tub soup and alum

Short mud
the fixed bloom

Pestered matches

Black wool

MEASURES TAKEN

Proving identity
the mirror reasons
a second face
obliged by the situation
of speech

One of one
and that
superfluous
culled elliptic
adds one on

The narrative
runs through proof
fastidious cordial
and blind timed
by quando's beating

Does and does not know
thing in manners
thing in chance
full of fragments to
mark the punctuated forecasts

Not a closed system
but an open-ended
compleynt and hails
of the anonymous
for sounding the you-apt

A NEW CHAIR

There is room for it
In the stubborn apprehension
Where hallelujah and inertia
Are not rivals but contain
A useful aptitude for vastness
One can go there and sit down

AN OTHER

There in that
And there again

Whether there
Or whether or

Something someone
Divides though two

Now are more
Than enough

By half

RUTHLESS CORNERS

Grammar re-educates myth
Has done so
When the paranoid presses
Distances always meet in the energy
One two three
Say it in French
Ein zwei drei
What the memory displaces
Is as have you had a No
For So as for Now again
The actual size of Behalf
Recusant traceries
The hand and its eye reach
Through the electricity and sweat
Have you an ear for the unroutine distances
And dust dances
The rose at the end of the dream
Is light reflected
Then absorbed

NB

1.

Words make me see things to say
That words don't say

2.

A mirror suspended in graygreen water
No
I'm tracking where I am
Another mirror in graygreen water

3.

The grasp in momentum that is thought
The grasp of momentum that is idea

NORTH

The space of origin
I've measured by the long blade
And raised it to the second power
With the deletion of the usual candor
Still-centered and wrapped in mud

And it's more mud
Along the edge of the first blade
And white paint along another
Grey wool through which to speak
Is draped from the third blade

The fourth gathers its light
From the re-imagined sheen
Of anything discrete or transparent
As relinquished here

FOUND AND LOST

Made aware of
The ever-changing chemicals of conjecture
What heritage is maintained in the loss of the real
As it begins again and again in simplicity

Tricked and blank
The arguments memory answers

With skin ever-thinner and
A good superstitious fact
On the the tip of the tongue
The crucial accumulates
Thick with hypotheses

Sensuous without terrain
The fox takes thought
We are there ignorant of the inadequate complexity
Of our galaxy
But measurements persist and terms from a moribund
Tradition based on the first horizon reassert the ignorance of order
Counting-out the equals of the instead

A FOR ISMS

The voice is a mistake natural to our intelligence.

Men do not want to learn even what is contradictory.

All our affections are produced in what only can be imagined.

Illusion is easily understood by what is clear.

Every house has need of distance.

Melancholy is better than justified enthusiasm.

Everything we can measure after so many wasted efforts becomes the foundation of ideology.

What holds us back is a love of remedies.

Pure duration or abstract extension make silence attentive but not for long.

When I speak of myself I varnish and vanish.

POEM

How the shallows tasted
When the shadows pulled away

Barely tolerated, I've come for your vocabulary
It will be a last sample . . . and so remain
A part of the neither . . . nor
Full of considerations of the larger variant
Marked by the pause where energy is steeped in ambition
Three dots flashing where you might wait within
Your choice of occasions acting out your thoughts
In concentric progressions: one here saying this and one there
Saying that the nameable is merely reassuring
Every delusion conforming to its aesthetic ideal
You lay claim to hearing the forgotten for the first time
But it hardly matters when as now brevity is shortness of breath
And finesse is the casually forgotten . . . gazing at the phone
While turning the pages of a manuscript
Where were those words last seen? Where heard?
Daring closeness instead of approximation
The foreshortened instead of the imminent
Seeking the universal's conquering uniformity in what balance
Might be achieved through mutually exclusive cohesion and
        interaction
The duplicate and immaculate

POST HOC PROPTER HOC

This place was a person
Now this place is displaced
The tide comes in

This place was
This place is a memory
Not a person

Some cities in New York
And Massachusetts
For a start

The tide runs out
The room is empty

The events that came before
Were an accounting

Words whose occasional syllables
Were replaced by numbers

To objectify a phrase by italic
Cuts an imprint to fissure

We've come this far through
New York Massachusetts and
Some places in Pennsylvania

To deepen the catch to come to
The negative of accomplishment
On horseback through town

So broken down with so exhibited
In echo and motley intervention
One step over the next

METRO

The locus of custom and hiatus
Seen in the me of you
A place of marathons steeps and trials
The maximum progress through circumstance
That the textures of scrutiny will allow
What is this what is being defined
The self-important exertions of attitude
A partially erased profile calling
That it would be a thing of the future
Is there some use for the purpose of this moment
Stumbling through the curdled light
Towards some previously undisclosed syllable
Threading crumbs of music through memoranda
And vicious disclosures about criteria
Enough to form an entire government out of amnesiacs
And unemployed zoo keepers
A world where citizens jump out at you and ask
"How long have you been on the back-burner?
I have all the money that matters if only you will help me
Fix this thing. But first please allow me to sharpen my pencil."

THE PREROGATIVE OF LIEDER

Here comes the question
The weather the sun and its shadows
The unauthorized itch that was scratched
Here comes the question

Intuition devotion before or after
An answer a question an answer
Surely far below but on high
Dramatic steams cast in the sulks

Means more clouds
Space interviews the rhyme
And the entire weight decides not
With a shall instead of a will

Momentarily a cormorant is the distance
Knotted no lurking in quietude
The floral pot-shaped voice is autumn
Papered over with a spectacle of grieving wit

The customary harping immersed in a story
Truthful to remembering the asking where
And telling backwards from the poured hymn
Propped along the winter and profane

PAGODA IN THE FOG

In the eyes
Better than we two
In the eyes
We three
The poet the translator and you

Landscape and music
Music the Harvard comma
Not where we listen
But where we wait

The lozenge or cartouche
In which the configurations
Of man horse cloud tree and
One or two other things help all involved
Determine just how many beans do make five

Balancing hate with envy
We get on with our lives
In as many different languages as
Certain irresistible frames of reference
Will compel
How much do you feel like working today
How much do you want to see the light
The distance in miles is still
The distance in a glance
The door opening
Erases all rhythms

THE UNSETTLING

Nothing and its twin
The face I put on thought
That turns its face away
To divide the efforts
And avoid misunderstandings
And tedious aspirations
Who are you—I don't want to know
That completion rusting in its accuracy
Is enough for the outward
The corrupted
The parallel rhythm ending in some fragmented
Apprehension you would have me understand
You would allow while engaging the preferred part
Of what I only seem to believe

ANY WONDER

Stubborn assertions rise into the murmurs
Strivings accumulate never to be realized
All part of the apprehensions of invention

The narcotic fanfare of unpleasant luxuries
Moves in fantasies of stratagem
Desperation's enthusiastic aspect

A headache glued to the newspaper
Grey on yellow smothers the signalled poise
Measures the peripheries iridescent in the deep shadows

The book is on the calendar
The book is in the calendar
This bracketed by then—not the weather but the heat

The sun white as an aspirin
The moon pink as a pig
Both given to the urban patience confirmed in its groan

The inconsolable is weighted with a sturdy
But impaired ego—but then there is that
Lathe-turned look we give a victim

Answers to answers blithe as the *uh* in spur

CALABRESE

I was young and from the south
A burden of bad options
Patient rambles or a million landscapes
Nothing else to offer

My salutations slip into pleasure
You've more than likely suggested
To yourself that you watch your step
So all I can do is try again

How many melodies and postscripts
Stalled in the damp
How many sharp edges
Under my bulky robes

DEEP IN THE OUTCOME

I gather and savor what came to be
Through the benevolent monotony of major commotions—
Changing clouds hooked on a wilderness of instincts
The shine and its tangents gradually applied to a decision of
    fundamental tatters
Clever as music with its extended nevertheless badgering the
    res rerum of precision
Out of the webs of dead ends and distracted oracles—their
    accusations honed
On the chewed lips of the politely-intuiting planning their scatter

You told me something but I can't remember what it was though it
    had a hand
In swelling the sea with the affection of its superior merit and
    pedestrian consequence
Trying to puzzle it out even now I'm left with little more than a sense
    of somber revery
And a species of rudimentary grammar meant to charm me out of
    a few pints of ink
Another morning in the republic waiting for the rain and preparing
    for elaborations
The first instinct was to recoil from the view—no that was some
    thing left to memory
A shabby canvas of limelit pines connect desire and remorse to the
    jinxy fable

Opening the dialogue with the words of the law and to a pledge
    of heckles
Well to hell with that and this that and the other—get away from
    me
There's a dead fly on your tongue and I certainly never believed
Those were voices in your head that was just the money talking
    and the assertions
Of wild and cultivated disdain grasping the opportunity to use the
    word blandishment

Instead of biting off the words with my teeth and tongue I kept
    them
Coming from the back of my throat like a man with a new face

First came the magnetic layer goofy with trompe l'oeil and easy
    sympathy but wanton
With fire torn from caprice I danced naked with the quoted
    confusion growing upside down
The same remarkable precipitate that enameled the ship-shape has
    snared the hummingbird
Something put aside for solemn opinion and enough dollars to make
    it seem worthwhile
You can't always get what you want but sometimes you can get what
    some po' bastard didn't need
With grim resolution they have inscribed let's go on the head of a
    bleeding man
After a few cigarettes we decide maybe it's not such a bad idea

DOCUMENT

Like something larger and it glows
In front of the intricate and maudlin bounty
Brittle attachments passing freely through the indifference
What is this and how did it get here
Complex ways to lose the struggle to change the price one pays
Plaits of the dead upon the bleak
Salvage your dilemma

Can you come back with the words made with a mechanism
Suspended in the manoeuvres of separation
You ask me what I want and I tell you
All you can see
The incantation and practice of reason continues in the dark
Painted distant in the moan just bearable—the part of the answer
That starts with no but ends with shovels and a liar

Corrupt arenas graphic and investigating the nonschematic fit to
    memories
The genre makes a polemic of the arbitrary
The mimetic capacity to perceive and reproduce similarities in
    deritualized valors
More objects in the saying than objections in the said
All over the way and profanely intricate and inclined to reveal
    and continue
Huddling together to disturb nothing
A worthy secret printed on the deception

ELEGY FOR THE NUMB

for Jim Brodey, his shade

What's puzzling you is the alleviation
Of these loosening portions—so

Introcue the tracks

This is the harsh ledge of cancellation
Turned into the lining of a name

First further

Suspicion's dragon eats the rope
So you can't get here from here
Best you can do is dim-fix the harvest
And kick somebody's ass

These are the allotments of the regal motes
There's a man here somewhere to tell you

A burnt pearl lurks in a heart of stone

And now this

Purely personal

He dips his fire into the wattage twelve words at a time

HALF-HEARD

To be primary
Only threadless warmth
A line of questions instead

Very basic and taciturn
Forlorn as the undulations of November
Not so much indolent as casually migratory

All the trivial hues finding their
Respective grays
Dull interpretations of memory
Jangle the intonings of drowse

The three worlds are still awake
Peculiar and solemn
Neither sensible nor of ancient accent
And nothing more

JOVE II

The tippy-toe lurchings of the midnight shambler
Are winding-up this sordid vignette
With an eye on its melancholy possibilities
Charcoal and cerise up against the lilac data
Who died and left him bandanna'd and clairvoyant
Puts a though in any thought of a straight answer
Let's have a prelude recondite with possibilities
Respite says live and let live even if the sun don't shine
Intimate with the smoke of manna and nagging enigmas
Looks like the prudent are here with the plaster

Tequila! Ramses! and chiffon!—an eclogue
In a paper bag tightly fastened with a frayed rubberband
Only longevity can protect the evil of your intentions
Weaving thunder with casual advice
And attributing your moods to an unknown artist
Boas in the lumber and filthy marvels at the crater
Immortal scalper of nervous manufacture! gaze a while
The blossoming trees charm the parachutists
Animal dreams go tongue to retina availed of whistled solos
For the French versions in the more scenic small towns

I'll never forget Dolores—her trench coat and lotions
There was every chance her tongue was an hour long
Some people claim she died of salt but I know it was her own
    damn fault
Electrocutions in taxicabs and the no joke poke heaven's overdue
Like a barnacle memorizing every sentiment backwards
Viva the streets! Pompeii is forging ahead and expiating its stammer
Crushed by the dimpled vigor of the age of music
The elephant can still find reason to smile
Forgiveness is on tour with a left-handed misprint
All the words for time are on my side

SUMMER LINES FOR ALEXANDRE

Gravity's leap is made known to the amateur when he staggers
A grammar of anecdotal darkness and hiatus

There was no first step after all
For which there was a precedent

It is the counterpoint that is vulnerable
Its vigilance is one eye on the horizon and one eye on the gesturing
    tense

Playing with the intricate tremors that turn into ideas one begins
    to feel
Nostalgic for what the complexities of grammar can be made
    to swallow

Tufted geometries and lichen-covered entablature
Red sky and white clouds as the crow flies aperture to aperture

The menace returns and this time he is whistling
Just this and the rustle of leaves are ceremony enough

It's in the narrow place that the survivor writes his manual
That, my friend, is heft in his grin and there's nothing else to call it

The profound gropings of a conspiratorial glamour
Flavor the benign mysteries of luck and ordinary inclination

Counting the stars for a few minutes and then dancing with the
    vast digit
Breathing is optional when we speak of this and its jeté

Through the panoramic Ô in hôtel then stride towards
The explosions with a stone in one hand and a brick in the other

Fully prepared for outrage and intimacy

HOURS HALL
for Hart Crane

Hedron for headroom notches the water step
Roentgen's trailing dot pinning the outline
Implacable neon by the sheaf

Riffed further from the wall's chisel
Are reef vaults and wicks of salt true to the rainbow's
Bulking the drop to span several pages

Diamond scrapers between the wedge and the dirt
Chop hoist the hammer clotting a grip on the grim
Oval slogans are static in the slam

Tractors stripe the gate and offer distances
Smokestacks in the equations between the holes
Hammer the nines in solution

Solid cherry is the ratio of spider to pathwood
It speaks to the penitential angle puzzling the eye-man
They end in a pan of enameled carbon marked with white integers

Nothing living that long engages the edge
Only tempo under the dry lip and the horn's rifling
When the weather changed

Submergence for threnody and an asterisk for genitals
Prisoners on the road and a polyphony of plumage in the arcade
Make four corners for the goblin scam

I think monsieur is familiar with the vertical keyboard
And the austere balance that exacts its shallows
Noon's fugue scratched on the lid

An axiom for calm is only what's offered
Intent and arrogance in the cut maps
Animal days in the leap

WE FOREGO MIMICRY

Thrift alone for meaning ceases
As this then starts from the middle out
The primitive halcyon required

Unpeopled knowledge waiting for creatures
Erect reactions
In a comic mode outside the cave
Is it architecture

Not the mountain but the thrown shaft
The describer to the real
Transfixing the included reflection
That's at last made to count

The foreignness of the syllable
And the visible
Watched in prolonged alleviation
Of ever-changing epigram

MONKEY BONES

The mysterious diminuendos of self-reproach
In a lap of shrouded dabble
There is a solitude better than comfort
To sound the approach of an ending
Will power elicits no further description
One is left for your pleasure
Fingerprints confide

POEM

1.

Abuse the differences and a whiteness remains in the margins
The several voices to the distances of otherness
Word for word the figures ask nothing
This exaggerates without thinking
Fulfills what remains incomplete
Like an echo
Definition brought to something as complex as a hole

2.
The motionless expanse of consequence
Alternative star of the multitude
Its edge defaults in the mirrored play of voyage
To sustain the word given its attentive modulations
The affection of the mechanism for revery
Exhaling through the teeth before giving shape to its sound
The logic of its rhythm bargains under the tongue

3.
These are the long particles that embrace
The fragmentation of the voices
Notes red notes and blue with many flags that answer
Wrapping the wind from a column of words
The spent stretch arguing from its found space
This is what has been reached this is what has been given
Its collected absence hanging from the lips

4.
After responding there is something further
Made of loss in the up-to-now of consequence
Inside the response
More attentive to the distraction
And the several voices of the indispensible crisis
Caught in mid-syllable

WHAT THE POSSE WOULD POSSESS

Let the day begin again
With only an occasional sound

Remote and agog as the frozen rose
These chairs take up no space

Machina ex deo
Just for color and smart sunshine

Dust disappears to enter the diamonds
In the oceanic sense of egregious

Statues are carved but never erected
We hasten down only to find the studios abandoned

Those are fish scales
Not mother of pearl in the moonlight

You fool
Whither those miming Valhalla

Day-glo ritmeester coronas charm the grins
In the warp of blind irony

The illusion knows about things
The illusionist doesn't

SIGNATURES

The terrible sanity of the eternal voices
Singing their schnell und Ruhe unter den fleet billowings
By bugler and knuckled keyboard
Earning the approval of
The moon as it lengthens its neck
The bland host of our edification and rescue

Addressing the symmetrical lump
Through a door to a scherzo
I must and if I do as well as I must
And if I do then what will be nothing more than thoughtless
Weaker ears have turned those anxieties into immortal energy
Calm but not intimate and with enough vastness to be of no use

Gone off on a journey only to cross a stream
Bright costumes and hunting dogs
Turn the episodes full of speculative swoons
Into zoos of peril and cracker-barrel animism
The miracles trudge the secrets are just a reminder
A light from the turret turns the brine to saffron

Advancing its habit-shaking aspirations
Envy's mail has blistered the eye
Who says it's a baffling fable and who says which whisper
Holds the immortal sneer that ennobles the distraction
From that pursuit spoken of in the first mood of careless temper
Singing and singing restless and attentive

SOME OF NONE

Drones of the simulacrum
Conceiving words in the sheltered crouch
No alternative coherences
Only the unconsolable certainty of light

Single maker of the shoving bloom
And smutted fragrance
Loose projections and pineapple talc
Instinctive shadows desert its fictive barbs

Fed on what two could share
Sets the isolation to conjuring
The imminence of a third
Tomorrow was never another day

THE ADJECTIVE

Posing in the care of the eye
That's where we found you
Privileged in the cheeks and
As these things go—long in the tooth

Hunkered against the wall with the real *however*
One of those with one foot in and one foot on
The lion's throat you're a
Stitch in the pulp of hides

All you need is love *zum beispiel*
Love is all you need
Memory's shakedown for the endless vig
Push push—do you like it like this

Unabashed and anxious licking
The sweat of a slave off your upper lip
Unwinding the cracking nag of time to a stare
This is the hang-on that belongs to no one else

THE BUILT SHADOW

Sure of much that had better
be right sure of less that had a better
chance of more than was expected
Shouted through the taking place
to the place it had taken
when there's nothing to lose you
make do with what was lost

THE DIGNITY TO EXPLAIN

Propitious the ambassador and the interlocutor
Struggle with the remuneration—a seabird's feathers
On the blade of a knife . . . You pretend
To touch me with a different agenda—it gets you a little
Attention but without Miss Laura where would you be now?

Gigantic wings crushing the atmosphere
Turning the air blue with their effort—
Have you come this far to see about me?
I have a rhythm to unravel—it seems little enough . . .
But when it's done in the sun it takes more than a pair of hands.

It's true—true enough—but I'm not sure in the telling.
There was the wind outside and the amazing absence it created.
It took nothing for granted and from where I stood
It took everything with it that wasn't nailed down.
The best defined pieces created an enclosure for the empty-handed.

The necessary skies were a blessing returned. What else could
    be seen?
Serious laughter—deliberate and well timed between parables . . .
The light on the slopes unlocking the guesswork made it seem like
    a plan
Was in the offing with something more than forbearance at its center.
Only the inaccuracies of the clay model made it all seem contrived.

A situation in infinity—not a stratagem—has some bearing on this
    fickleness.
This is where it has been put . . . that much I do remember. That
    much I can say.
Again you want to ask what else? Are you aspiring to remorse or is
    that an Etruscan mask?
The erratic path of the old comet is made of ice and iron. With a
    few words
You can wave it on its way for another thousand years.

THE MONTHS

You change you juggle you choke
A story per

This is the moment that nothing describes

A linear trick

Change heard [23 years pass] heard Change
How the eyes work across words

The route filed with a membrane of water

The rain wears its contracts rep-resented insignia

Two by one
Two by two

Separation of desperation's decoy
From its contacts

One or one and two at a time

The selection from the inside

Always moving
All in every which way

Little else

For balance

Phrased in magnetic north
Crystal duplicated in decay

THE SHELL

Torn from the presumption
No longer wary
But still not quite yours
The answer still starting "That's how"
And achingly inscribed in pencil
Slipped in where something else rubbed off
The climate is no longer careful
Combed out of a long familiarity
These are the chambers of cognition occupying
From where you sit the middle distance
Never close enough more like the smell of garlic
Under the nails—an old acquaintance become a lost object
There is more time for negative thoughts before
The glow builds its insistence
Something about the affording quite plain in its approach
Later it's a soft peg good for fixing a horizon to be disconnected
And after that an obvious though earnest commitment
To coming back tomorrow with something earmarked for
        authorization
Like a talisman the setting sun has been imprinted with numerals
That flake into the night sky—equal to the worst
On either side of the means to the calm of loss
Still with the growing grass I'm going to miss you
Obstinate here at the rim of the infinite burden
We spend the night together a muzzle on diligence
Warmed by the friction of reconstructed anonymity
Nothing to be learned from irony at this point
Even the passerby one of us would become knows that
Millions have been wooed by the gossamer blab
But now when the drum throbs it's just time for a new sense
        of merit
To overtake the vicarious swing the pendulum makes

TO BE OF

Complex stimulation of the span of faith
Inflammatory distractions, cheap feelings, unsparing pianos
Work half a dozen words for it

A sentimental hauteur contorts the face
A time for antecedents soon passes
Chastened axioms, mud on the boots, blood on the balloons

So many down on their knees up in the clouds
They make for pertinence and epoch
Crimson glares inspire the attitude

Vernacular intrusions spread-eagle on a routine
There's a lush tottering in the metonymic disdain
Muffled sorrows are haunted by sunsets and potted scruples

A resignation so prehensile it can wind a clock
Calls out across the swarthy real estate its
Clammy terraces of orchestrated antagonism offer

A new life under cinnamon boughs
All the tease in China fills my amphora behind a shady tree
Larousse and Harrap by the bushel

FRAGMENT

What would I rather have now that a choice was made

Listening at night
I see the private words rendered
Until there's light and it reaches
The consent and welter of impulse

The mood survives its quarter-turn
Combinations undulating to the pull
That would become the main point
The basic principle only half-meant

A perfect transparency
There is nothing left now
A beast of burden dead on its feet
The myths still

The calm center of a certain possible world

A MODERN INSTANCE

The metaphor of proportions
The icon of analogy

Enunciates an extensive list
Struck out of certain verbs

Naming the knot at the source
Comes ascribing comes next

Revolves hidden
In the quibble

Tangle to tangle
The motion in the drift

Its reach along
Its while through

Companions outcaught and withcaught
Over the light

To the crease
The distance back to measure

The version reproduced there
And its singling

The ingredient turned in its commerce
The balance cannot validate

The fold in the formula
Presented shadows their situations

A record of the intuitive endeavors
Serendipitous at the graft

That pull is its practiced options
Isolated in ascribed motive

The brag of a straw grid
Against what slowly computes

The letterings of another
Rare prediction

The rift in the perspective
Lined by the eye at its highest point

But below is syncopated vertigo
Up from down the only technicality

How it was
As far as the rim

Its tentative reach along
Its random insistence the while through

The lost city in the picture
Its trees reflected in the effect

Gauging the calm allure
Hearing the tin echoing in the g's

Counted-out directed
Blank legacy for the mark

The height the weight the color
Compete with the exchanges

The prank and the debt
Meant to make

SPECULATIONS ON A GRIN

The gaze collapses
Become a schema for withdrawal
Better to tell a lie
And look confused
Adopt a tilt towards
Restructuring anxieties

A mere inclination
Above not level with
The exacerbation of the catch caught
It prints its part of this
Only recognizes its part of this
A bizarre combination of extra-virgin
And salacious typographical error
Most narrow
Where the blunt edge turns

Tendering that resignation that goes down refusing
To distinguish between hundreds per centimeter and thousands
Another carping fragment pushed across under a date
If and day all and month if indeed and year

IL GIARDINO DI POPULI

At work on the orders of interest
The sputtered evidence of once
And never again—another word for until
Thinking how it probably worked before
But for whom and after all why not
The am and in held in line by stamina

What have you forgotten
That's what I would remember and say here
Avoiding the recreational repair called for by interpretation
Its strict asides speak of a dormant contraption
Yesterday's someday and tomorrow's traces
Broken barrels of books for a dollar

Paradigms and the erasures of carrion
Where where how covert where's its shadow
All that's offered by a necessary gaze is
A jagged line all the way to the horizon
The public identification and private disclosures
At best a few thin suggestions spiced by disclaimers

Immersion and artifact
There seems to be a foregone conclusion
Looking and talking and their amalgam conspiracy
Leaves rocks trees the fences and cinder paths all intrusive
What have you brought me in bringing me here
Dismantling the divining pressures and calling them ambitions

SANCTION

I must warn you
The situation isn't what it used to be
When no one asked who I was
I looked like I belonged
As long as I stayed inside
An awareness of promising instants
Cautelous affections
Quodlibetically constituted

Now instead
Comes an anonymous translation
Hodie sicut semper . . . limestone
Handwritten words where the sun hangs
Natural parts and culpable beginnings
Offering safe conduct as far as the unraveled vines

LIP TRAP AT TERRA NUOVA

1. A BLOW TO THE HEAD

I have become speculation
Breathless matters and exhausted innocence ~~in alternation~~
Consequence neither patient nor remote

Lightning and tedium
Giving way to mottos
Endless confusions fed by glances

Dancing and quarreling
Proof ~~and an hour later further proof~~
The abrasions of common sense

It's mine but now it's in your hands
~~Reduced by your theft to another educated moment~~
Colorless and self-illustrating

Neither real simple nor simple nor real
A little human effect ~~that rang false~~
The worried contribution of a technical amateur

~~Who stealthy as a lizard~~
~~Has invested in a misbegotten plan~~

2. A MAP OF THE CITY

This laughter is requisite
It proves the truth

~~Night's~~ unanticipated luster
Settles in the fragment of a pause

~~Heat and dust~~ equal to any situation
I have been given

~~An exceptional~~ register of squandered extracts
Who here where there what now

The risk to keep anything more than anything else
Thicker words under the percolations of chagrin

Only ~~for me~~ the invisible flatness
Massing under its jumps

~~After all the the squinting sonatas~~
~~Coming in my direction from a friend~~

A sound in the courtyard a hum and then three short notes
Manikins ~~wrapped in the curtains of the arcade~~

A word in the face
Nothing on the tongue

3. BRAVO SPIKE

I dreamt the lost word *after* the perfect number
First things first

Increment wondering
~~Inclement wandering~~ Increment wandering

~~He says~~ He explains
The paradoxes with his head

Platforms and mirrors
~~Along the spiders' miles~~

~~Folk blurs rendered sentry~~
Empty the ancient of its shambles

Charred replicas and sunset tattoos provide
~~Only~~ occult ochre and picayune

The radio complains of thought cures
Verbatim works for money

Now everyone's looking for verbs in the porridge
~~Shouts at the shadows and whispers at the snakes~~

In the cities of regalia
And the townships of hunch

Anxious minorities ~~with guns and binoculars~~
Gather on the hills

4. NEW RELICS

Guest of the object
~~And the rhymes that taste~~
Part of the until ~~relative to~~
The rest of it

Something once used for ninety minutes
But always there
Made for stillness found
~~Already old and not well~~

Lifted ~~in~~ at under the music
Come to ritual
Bone cloth wood shapes
Of the remainder

Departed ~~with~~ what was left
Perfect enough ~~to inscribe~~
A use arrested ~~with some new verses~~
Versus what avoided the identity of its loss

5. BRICKYARD BOULEVARD

No expressions ~~types presentations~~
Must have been taught on a
Rickety stage the faces in the fumes

~~Loom at the moons~~
This raw context ~~its glamour~~
Reaches the sensings of humor

Hard as the fraction
Bad bones and immortal
~~Sniffed snipped~~ chords lighthandedness

Popucalculated areas and the levitation
Of incongruous stuff
Predeceased by the adroit impression

~~These langsam offerings~~
Conflicting questions no landscapes
No null no void just

Sly urges
The planes and plains of the vice versa
Paper mud and light

The half-hesitant destiny
The numb principle
The lithe paraphrase

ROOF BOOKS

Andrews, Bruce. **EX WHY ZEE.** 112p. $12.95.

Andrews, Bruce. **Getting Ready To Have Been Frightened**. 116p. $7.50.

*Andrews, Bruce. **R & B.** 32p. $2.50.

Benson, Steve. **Blue Book**. Copub. with The Figures. 250p. $12.50

Bernstein, Charles. **Islets/Irritations**. 112p. $9.95.

Bernstein, Charles (editor). **The Politics of Poetic Form**. 246p. $12.95; cloth $21.95.

Brossard, Nicole. **Picture Theory**. 188p. $11.95.

Child, Abigail. **From Solids**. 30p. $3.

Davies, Alan. **Active 24 Hours**. 100p. $5.

Davies, Alan. **Signage**. 184p. $11.

Davies, Alan. **Rave**. 64p. $7.95.

Day, Jean. **A Young Recruit**. 58p. $6.

Dickenson, George-Thérèse. **Transducing**. 175p. $7.50.

Di Palma, Ray. **Raik**. 100p. $9.95.

Doris, Stacy. **Kildare**. 104p. $9.95

Dreyer, Lynne. **The White Museum**. 80p. $6.

Edwards, Ken. **Good Science.** 80p. $9.95.

Eigner, Larry. **Areas Lights Heights**. 182p. $12, $22 (cloth).

Gizzi, Michael. **Continental Harmonies**. 92p. $8.95.

Gottlieb, Michael. **Ninety-Six Tears**. 88p. $5.

Grenier, Robert. **A Day at the Beach**. 80p. $6.

Hills, Henry. **Making Money**. 72p. $7.50. VHS videotape $24.95.
   Book & tape $29.95.

Hunt, Erica. **Local History**. 80 p. $9.95.

Inman, P. **Criss Cross**. 64 p. $7.95.

Inman, P. **Red Shift**. 64p. $6.

Lazer, Hank. **Doublespace**. 192 p. $12.

Mac Low, Jackson. **Representative Works: 1938–1985**. 360p. $12.95, $18.95 (cloth).

Mac Low, Jackson. **Twenties**. 112p. $8.95.

McCaffery, Steve. **North of Intention**. 240p. $12.95.

Moriarty, Laura. **Rondeaux**. 107p. $8.

Neilson, Melanie. **Civil Noir**. 96p. $8.95.

Pearson, Ted. **Planetary Gear**. 72p. $8.95.

Perelman, Bob. **Face Value. 72p. $6.

Perelman, Bob. **Virtual Reality**. 80p. $9.95.

Piombino, Nick, **The Boundary of Blur**. 128p. $13.95

Robinson, Kit. **Balance Sheet.** 112 p. $9.95.

Robinson, Kit. **Ice Cubes**. 96p. $6.

Scalapino, Leslie. **Objects in the Terrifying Tense Longing from Taking Place.** 88p. $9.95.

Seaton, Peter. **The Son Master**. 64p. $4.

*Sherry, James. **Part Songs**. 28p. $10.

Sherry, James. **Popular Fiction**. 84p. $6.

Silliman, Ron. **The Age of Huts. 150p. $10.

Silliman, Ron. **The New Sentence**. 200p. $10.

Silliman, Ron. **N/O**. 112 p. $10.95.

Templeton, Fiona. **YOU—The City**. 150p. $11.95.

*Ward, Diane. **Never Without One**. 72p. $5.

Ward, Diane. **Relation**. 64p. $7.50.

Watten, Barrett. **Progress**. 122p. $7.50.

*Out of Print**Rare (inquire for price)

Discounts: 2 – 4 books, 20%; 5 or more, 40%.

For ordering, send check or money order in U.S. dollars to:

SEGUE FOUNDATION, 303 East 8th Street, New York, NY 10009